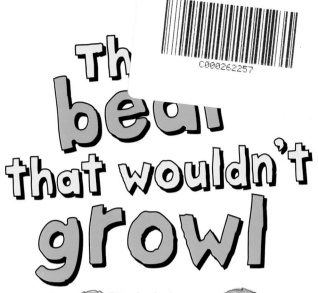

The bear that wouldn't growl

Written and illustrated

by

Shoo Rayner

Heinemann

We all know that grizzly bears growl.
Well, this is a story about a
grizzly bear that would not growl.
The bear was called Bella.

Bella was a happy bear and she never, ever growled. Not even when she was asked to do things that she didn't like doing.

When Bella's mum asked her to clean her cave, Bella would just give her a big smile and say, 'Yes, Mum.'

When Bella's dad asked her to be quiet and to sit still at the table, Bella would just give him a big smile and say, 'Yes, Dad.'

And when Bella's brother, Bruno,
wanted all the toys to play with,
Bella would just give him a big smile
and say, 'Yes, Bruno.'

One day, Bella's mum said to Bella's dad, 'Bella is happy all the time and she never growls. She will not grow up to be a grizzly bear.'

So they took Bella to a grizzly bear school.

'They will show her how to growl,' they said.

At school Bella had to go to growling classes. Her teacher tried and tried to make her growl, but it was no good. Bella just smiled all the time.

The teacher gave a report to
Bella's mum and dad. It said,

Grizzly School

Report

I'm sorry to say that
Bella will never be
a grizzly bear because
she won't growl.
However, she would
make a good teddy bear.

Bella's mum and dad were sad.
They said to Bella, 'We have tried to
show you how to be a grizzly bear
but it is no good. You never growl.
You will have to go away and
live on your own in the forest.
We'll see if that makes you growl.'

So Bella went off to live in the forest
on her own.

She made her new home in a
little cave. Bella liked living there.

When Bella was hungry she went
for a walk in the forest.
There was lots to eat in the forest
and Bella was always happy.
She never growled at anything.

Bella's cave was by a river.
As the fish swam by, Bella would
catch them and eat them.

But Bella liked eating honey best of all
and by her cave was a giant bee hive.
So Bella was very happy and she
never growled at anything.

One day, Bella's family came to see
her new home.

'This cave is very cold,' growled
Bella's mum.

Bella stopped smiling.

'Well, I like it,' she said.

'This cave is very little,' growled
  Bella's dad.
  Bella was cross.
'Well, I like it,' she said.

'I don't like this cave,' growled Bruno.
'It's no good at all.'
Now Bella was very cross.

'This is my home and I like it,'
said Bella, and she let out the
biggest growl that Mum, Dad and
Bruno had ever heard.
'Bella!' they all said. 'You can growl!
You **are** a grizzly bear!'